C000138417

Nadakkave, Kozhikode, Kerala
www.insightpublica.com
e-mail: insightpublica@gmail.com
Title: **Little Grey Hare**
Boris Zakhoder
Translated by K.M.Cook-Horujy
Illustrated by V.Chizhikov
Insight Publica Edition: September 2021

ISBN 978-93-5517-039-2
Printed and Published by
InsightinPublica Printers & Publishers Pvt Ltd.

₹ 240

# Little Grey Hare

## Boris Zakhoder
Translated by **K.M.Cook-Horujy**
Illustrated by **V.Chizhikov**


# Wee Little Havroshechka

## Russian Fairy Tale
Translated by **Irina Zheleznova**
Illustrated by **O.Korotkova**
Page:23

Once upon a time there was a hare called Little Grey Hare who had a friend called Tadpole. Little Grey Hare lived in a forest glade, and Tadpole lived in a pond.

When they met, Tadpole would wiggle his tail and Little Grey Hare would drum his paws. He talked to Tadpole about carrots, and Tadpole talked to him about waterweed, and it was great fun.

One day Little Grey Hare went to the pond, but Tadpole wasn't there. Not a sign of him!

A little frog was sitting on the bank.

"Hey, Froggy!" Little Grey Hare said. "Have you seen my friend Tadpole anywhere?"

"No, I haven't," sniggered Froggy, chuckling to himself. "Tee, hee, hee!"

"There's nothing to laugh about," cried Little Grey Hare. "My best friend's got lost, and all you can do is laugh! Silly thing!"

"I'm not silly," said Froggy. "You're the one who's silly! Fancy not recognising your own friend. It's me."

"What do you mean-you?" asked Little Grey Hare, puzzled.

"I'm your old friend Tadpole!"

'You?" Little Grey Hare cried in astonishment. 'You can't be! Tadpole had a tail, but you haven't. You don't look a bit like him!"

"I may not look like him, but I am him all the same," Froggy replied. "It's just that I've grown up and turned into a frog. That's what always happens."

"Fancy that," said Little Grey Hare. "So it always happens, does it?"

"Of course it does. Everyone changes when they grow up. From a grub into a mosquito, from

spawn into a fish, and from a tadpole into a frog, everyone knows that! There's

even a little rhyme about it.

Tadpoles whether fast or slow

Into little frogs do grow"

And at this point Little Grey Hare decided to believe him.

"Thanks for telling me," he said. "I'll have to think about that."

And so they parted.

Little Grey Hare went home and asked his mother:

"Will I soon grow up, Mum?"

"Oh, yes, dear, very soon," said his mother. "When the leaves turn yellow, you'll be big. We, hares, grow quickly!"

"And what will I turn into?"

"What do you mean - turn into?" His mother was puzzled.

"What will I be when I grow up?"

"Oh, that's easy," said his mother. "You'll be a big handsome hare, like your father."

"We'll see about that," said Little Grey Hare.

And off he ran to find what he would like to turn into.

"I'll take a look at everybody who lives in the forest and turn into the one I like best," he thought.

The saucy little creature!

As he walked through the forest, birds sang all around.

"That's nice," thought Little Grey Hare. "Why don't I turn into a bird? I could just fly about singing songs. I like singing, but we, hares, sing so quietly that nobody can hear us."

No sooner had he thought this, than he saw a bird sitting on a branch. A gorgeous bird, bigger than a hare, with fine black feathers. It was singing a lovely song.

"Boo, boo, boo! Chuff-chuffick!"

"Aunty Bird!" called Little Grey Hare. "What's your name?"

"Chuff-chuffick!" replied Wood-grouse, for him it was.

"Uncle Wood-grouse, how can I become a bird?"

"Chuff-chuffick!" replied Wood-grouse.

"I want to turn into a bird," Little Grey Hare explained. But all he got in reply was:

"Boo, boo, boo! Chuff-chuffick!"

"Can't he hear properly?" thought Little Grey Hare. He was just about to go up to the bird when he heard footsteps.

"A hunter! Look out, Uncle Chuffick!" cried Little Grey Hare. He hardly had time to hide in the bushes, before some shots rang out. Bang! Bang!

Little Grey Hare peeped out. There was a lot of smoke and feathers floating about. The hunter had shot off some of Uncle Wood-grouse's tail.

So much for Uncle Chuffick!

"No," thought Little Grey Hare. "I don't want to be a wood-grouse. They sing nice and loudly, but they don't hear properly. No wonder they lose their tails. We hares always

keep our ears pricked, on the alert."

So off he ran, singing a little song to keep his courage up, the Brave Hare's Song. This is how it went.

Five, four, three, two, one!

Along came a Hunter with his gun!

All of a sudden out Little Hare popped,

Hunter raised his gun and shot!

Biff! Baff! Goodness me!

Hunters climbing up a tree!

Singing made him feel nice and cheerful.

Then he saw Squirrel hopping from branch to branch.

"She does hop well," thought Little Grey Hare. "Just as well as me! Perhaps I should be a squir-rel."

"Squirrel, Squirrel, come here!" he called.

Squirrel hopped down to the lowest branch.

"Hello, Little Grey Hare," she said. "What do you want?"

"Tell me what it's like being a squirrel, please," Little Grey Hare asked. "I'm thinking of becoming one."

"Oh, it's very nice indeed," said Squirrel. "We have a lovely time, hopping from branch to branch, cracking cones and nibbling nuts. Only we have a lot of work to do, like building nests and gathering mushrooms and nuts for the winter. Still you'll get used to that. Climb up here and I'll teach you the things a squirrel has to know!"

Little Grey Hare walked up to the tree, thinking: "So they have a lot of work to do... We hares don't have a care in the world. We don't build nests or dig holes..."

He started to climb up a tree, but he went all dizzy.

"No," he said. "I don't want to be a squirrel! We hares weren't made to go climbing trees!"

Squirrel laughed, tut-tutted and threw a cone at him.

Fortunately it missed.

On went Little Grey Hare until he came to a clearing where some little mice were doing somersaults. Little Grey Hare watched.

Suddenly they all turned and fled for their lives.

"Fox! Fox!" they squealed.

And sure enough there was Lady Fox with her fine fur coat, white bib, ears pricked and tail held high. A splendid sight!

"Surely they can't be afraid of such a fine lady," thought Little Grey Hare.

He walked out boldly, bowed and said:

"Good day, Lady Fox! May I ask you something?"

"Here's a saucy one!" Lady Fox exclaimed in surprise. "Alright, only hurry up. I don't waste words on the likes of you."

"It won't take a minute. Teach me how to be a fox. Tell me what it's like. I think you're marvellous!"

Lady Fox was very flattered.

"Well," she said. "I don't do anything special, just kill what I catch, and eat what I kill! That's all there is to it!"

This terrified Little Grey Hare, but he didn't show it, only wiggled his ears.

"So that's why everyone's afraid of you!" he said. "No, I won't be a fox. We hares never raise a paw against anyone else."

"A good thing too," said Lady Fox. "If hares turned into foxes, who would we, foxes, have to eat?"

And her big eyes glittered as she bared her teeth. Any minute now she would pounce on Little Grey Hare and that would be the end of him.

But Little Grey Hare was up and away even before she had finished talking! He said to himself, as he sped along: "Fancy her wanting to gobble up a live hare! That means if I were a fox I'd have to eat myself."

Little Grey Hare ran round the forest for a long time and saw all the animals. With the exception of the wolf, who was even crueller than the fox, he liked them all. But there was always something wrong with them.

He wanted to be a mouse, but they're so small, or a hedgehog, but they're so prickly. Nobody would stroke him, and hares like to be stroked. Or a beaver, but it was so wet in the river.

He almost decided to be a bear. Bear told him that he ate honey, and honey was even sweeter than carrots. But Little Grey Hare didn't want to sleep the whole winter away in his lair, sucking his paw.

"We, hares, can't do that," he said. "We were made to run about."

And on he ran until he came to a marsh in the forest.

Then he stopped short in amazement.

There stood a splendid Beast, as huge as can be, bigger than a bear, with long legs, two pairs of ears, as long as a hare's, and the kindest eyes you ever saw.

He stood there, munching grass and gnawing an aspen branch.

Little Grey Hare thought he was absolutely wonderful.

He bowed low to be Beast.

"Good day, Uncle," he said. "What is your name, please?"

"Good day, Little Grey Hare," said the giant. "My name is Elk."

"Why do you have two pairs of ears, Uncle?"

Elk laughed.

"You must have mistaken my antlers for ears," he said.

"Why do you need antlers?"

"To protect myself from enemies," said Elk. "From wolves and the rest of them."

"Oo, how marvellous!" said Little Grey Hare. "But what's it like being an elk?"

"Nothing special. We gnaw branches and munch grass."

18 Little Grey Hare

"Do you eat carrots?"

"Yes, carrots too, if we get hold of them."

"And you don't eat other animals?"

"Goodness me, no," Elk replied. "What an idea!"

This made Little Grey Hare like Elk even more.

"I'll be an elk," he thought.

"And you don't climb trees?" he asked.

"Certainly not! What for?"

"And you can run fast?"

"I should say so," Elk laughed.

"And you don't sleep in a lair in winter and suck your paw?"

"Who do you think I am, a bear?" Elk laughed.

Little Grey Hare made up his mind to be an elk.

But just in case he decided to ask one more question.

"Does it take long to be an elk?"

"No, not very long," said Elk. "You have to grow for five or six years, then you turn from a little elk into a real big one!"

This upset Little Grey Hare so much, he almost burst into tears.

"No," he said. "We, hares, can't take five years to grow up. Good-bye, Uncle Elk! I can't do it..."

"Good-bye, laddy," said Elk.

And Little Grey Hare ran off home.

On the way he passed the pond. There were yellow leaves floating on it now. Froggy was sitting on a large leaf. He had grown much bigger, of course. He was almost a fully-grown frog by now, but Little Brown Hare recognised him all the same.

"Hello, Tadpole that was!" he called.

He recognised Froggy, but Froggy did not seem to recognise him. He took fright and dived into the water.

Little Grey Hare was surprised. "What's the matter wit him?" he thought.

Froggy poked his head out of the water and said:

"Silly thing! Fancy giving people a fright like this!"

"You're the silly thing, not me," Little Brown Hare laughed. "Fancy you, Tadpole that was, not recognising your friends. It's me!"

"What do you mean - you?" Froggy asked, puzzled.

"It's your old friend, Little Grey Hare."

"Well, I never," said Froggy. "But you're not little anymore. You're a real Grey Hare now!"

And back into the water he dived.

Little Grey Hare looked into the water when the ripples had died down.

And he saw that he really had turned into a big handsome hare. Just like his father, with nice thick fur, strong paws, big eyes and the finest pair of ears you've ever seen!

And he drummed his paws with sheer delight.

# Wee Little Havroshechka

Translated by **Irina Zheleznova**
Illustrated by **O.Korotkova**

There are good people in the world and some who are not so good. There are also people who are shameless in their wickedness.

Wee Little Havroshechka had the bad luck to fall in with such as these. She was an orphan and these people took her in and brought her up only to make her work till she could not stand. She spun and wove and did the housework and had to answer for everything.

Now, the mistress of the house had three daughters. The eldest was called One-Eye, the second Two-Eyes, and the youngest Three-Eyes.

The three sisters did nothing all day but sit by the gate and watch what went on in the street, while Wee Little Havroshechka sewed, spun and wove for them and never heard a kind word in return.

Sometimes Wee Little Havroshechka would go out into the field, put her arms round the neck of her brindled cow and pour out all her sorrows to her.

"Brindled, my dear," she would say. "They beat me and scold me, they don't give me enough to eat, and yet they forbid me to cry. I am to have five poods of flax spun, woven, bleached and rolled by tomorrow."

And the cow would say in reply:

"My bonny lass, you have only to climb into one of my ears and come out of the other, and your work will be done for you."

And just as Brindled said, so it was. Wee Little Havroshechka would climb into one of the cow's ears, and come out through the other. And lo and behold!—there lay the cloth, all woven and bleached and rolled.

Wee Little Havroshechka would then take the rolls of cloth to her mistress who would look at them and grunt and put them away in a chest and give Wee Little Havroshechka even more work to do.

And Wee Little Havroshechka would go to Brindled, put her arms round her and stroke her, climb into one of her ears and come out of the other, pick up the ready cloth and take it to her mistress again.

One day the old woman called her daughter One-Eye to her and said:

"My good child, my bonny child, go and see who helps the orphan with her work. Find out who spins the flax and who weaves the cloth and rolls it."

One-Eye went with Wee Little Havroshechka into the woods and she went with her into the
fields, but she forgot her mother's command and
she lay down on the grass and basked in the sun.

And Wee Little Havroshechka murmured:
"Sleep, little eye, sleep!"

One-Eye shut her eye and fell asleep. While she slept. Brindled wove, bleached and rolled the cloth.

The mistress learned nothing, so she sent for Two-Eyes, her second daughter, and said to her:

"My good child, my bonny child, go and see who helps the orphan with her work."

Two-Eyes went with Wee Little Havroshechka, but she forgot her mother's command and she lay down on the grass and basked in the sun. And Wee Little Havroshechka murmured:

"Sleep, little eye! Sleep, the other little eye!"

Two-Eyes shut her eyes and dozed off. While she slept, Brindled wove, bleached and rolled the cloth.

The old woman was very angry and on the third day she told Three-Eyes, her third daughter, to go with Wee Little Havroshechka to whom she gave more work to do than ever.

Three-Eyes played and skipped about in the sun until she was so tired that she lay down on the grass. And Wee Little Havroshechka sang out:

"Sleep, little eye! Sleep, the other little eye!"

But she forgot all about the third little eye.

Two of Three-Eyes' eyes fell asleep, but the third looked on and saw everything. It saw Wee Little Havroshechka climb into one of the cow's ears and come out of the other and pick up the ready cloth.

Three-Eyes came home and she told her mother what she had seen.

The old woman was overjoyed, and on the very next day she went to her husband and said:

"Go and kill the brindled cow."

The old man was astonished and tried to reason with her.

"Have you lost your wits, old woman?" he said. "The cow is a good one and still young."

"Kill it and say no more," the wife insisted.

There was no help for it and the old man began to sharpen his knife.

Wee Little Havroshechka found out about it and she ran to the field and threw her arms round Brindled.

"Brindled, my dear," she said, "they want to kill you!"

And the cow replied:

"Do not grieve, my bonny lass, and do what I tell you. Take my bones, tie them up in a kerchief, bury them in the garden and water them every day. Do

not eat of my flesh and never forget me." The old man killed the cow, and Wee Little Havroshechka did as Brindled had told her to. She went hungry, but she would not touch the meat, and she buried the bones in the garden and watered them every day.

After a while an apple-tree grew up out of them, and a wonderful tree it was! Its apples were round and juicy, its swaying boughs were of silver and its rustling leaves were of gold. Whoever drove by would stop to look and whoever came near marvelled.

A long time passed by and a little time, and one day One-Eye, Two-Eyes and Three-Eyes were out walking in the garden. And who should chance to be riding by at the time but a young man, handsome and curly-haired and strong and rich. When he saw the juicy apples he stopped and said to the girls teasingly:

"Fair maidens! Her will I marry amongst you three who brings me an apple off yonder tree."

And off rushed the sisters to the apple-tree, each trying to get ahead of the others.

But the apples which had been hanging very low and seemed within easy reach, now swung up high in the air above the sisters' heads.

The sisters tried to knock them down, but the leaves came down in a shower and blinded them. They tried to pluck the apples off, but the boughs caught in their braids and unplaited them. Struggle and stretch as they would, they could not reach the apples and only scratched their hands.

Then Wee Little Havroshechka walked up to the tree, and at once the boughs bent down and the apples came into her hands.

She gave an apple to the handsome young stranger, and they were married soon after. From that day on she knew no sorrow, but lived with her husband in health and cheer and grew richer from year to year.

48 Wee Little Havroshechka

9 789355 170392